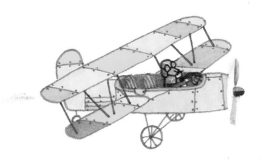

THOSE MAGNIFICENT SHEEP IN THEIR FLYING MACHINE

Peter Bently

David Roberts

ANDERSEN PRESS

The sheep on the hillside were munching away,
Much as they always did, day after day,
When suddenly something went —

ZOOM!

— overhead.

"Let's go and see what it is!" they all said.

So Lambert and Eunice and Marty and Mabs
And Old Uncle Ramsbottom, Bart, Ben and Babs
Skipped to the hilltop and saw down below . . .

Dozens of aeroplanes all in a row!
There were men with moustaches in goggles and spats
And ladies in splendidly colourful hats,
And jolly brass bands playing pom-diddle-dee.
"An air race! An air race!" the lambs cried with glee.

A bright yellow aeroplane stood nearby.
"How spiffing," said Eunice, "to fly in the sky!
No one will mind if we have a quick peep!"
So one-by-one into the plane jumped the sheep.

"Oh dear," muttered Mabs. "It's a bit of a squeeze.
But there's just enough room if you tuck up your knees."

"Move up, Ben!" said Eunice. But Ben couldn't budge,
So Old Uncle Ramsbottom gave him a nudge,
Which made him bump Lambert, who bonked into Babs,

Who banged into Marty, who bashed into Mabs,
Who bleated, "Oh bother!" and biffed against Bart —

Who butted a little green button marked START!

The engine went CHUGGITY-CHUGGITY-COUGH!
And Old Uncle Ramsbottom cried, "Let me off!"
But the plane quickly started to trundle downhill —
And faster and faster it trundled until . . .

Old Uncle Ramsbottom, Bart, Ben and Babs
And Lambert and Eunice and Marty and Mabs,
Caused all the people to gasp and to stare
As the bright yellow aeroplane took to the air!

"I say!" cried a gent with
a silver-topped cane.
"Some thieves in white
sweaters are taking my plane!"

"Ahhh!" cried the sheep as they swerved and they swooped.

"Oooh!" they all groaned as the plane loop-the-looped.

They did a steep nosedive and rolled a few rolls —

Then Old Uncle Ramsbottom grabbed the controls.

"Wa-hay!"

he exclaimed.

"What a lark!

What a thrill!

This beats eating grass on our boring old hill!
The world is our oyster!" he cried out in glee.
"Let's see a few sights!" And they all cried,

"Yippee!"

They can-canned in France

and flamencoed in Spain —

Till a furious bull chased them back to the plane.

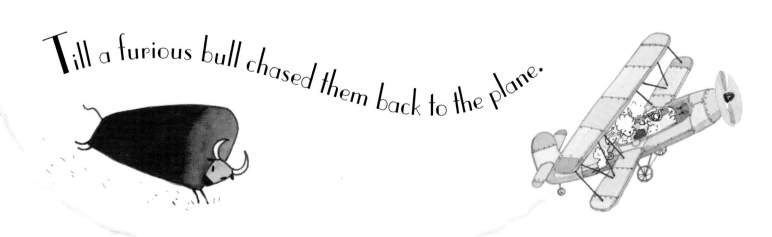

They flew over Egypt with rumbling tummies,
So they stopped for a picnic — and woke up some **mummies!**

In Tibet, little Ben found a mound of spaghetti.
He chomped a great mouthful —
"Run! It's a YETI!"

An old maharajah sat stroking his belly
And said, "Come for lunch at my palace in Delhi!"
But they soon scuttled back to the plane in a hurry
When they asked, "What's to eat?" and he said,

"Mutton curry!"

They sat on a log in a Florida swamp —
But the log in the swamp wanted something to chomp!

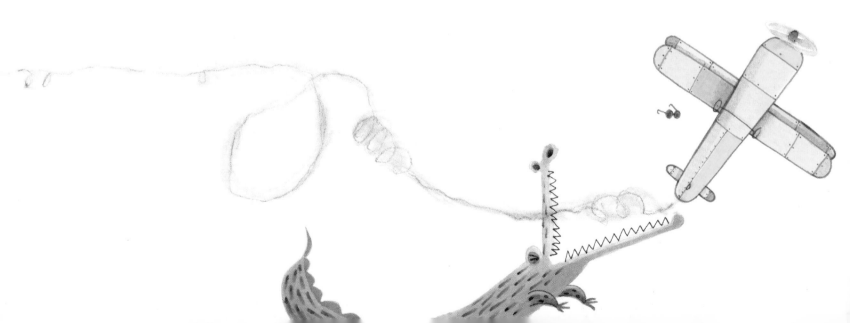

"Where next?" said old Ramsbottom. "Minsk? Timbuktu?
Saskatchewan? Zanzibar? Kalamazoo?
What about Chile? Or China? Or Rome?"
But the other sheep all shook their heads and said: "Home!"

"We miss the old field! We miss the old hill! We miss chewing grass! We miss standing still! Travel is fun! Every person should try it!

But there's no place like home if you want peace and quiet."

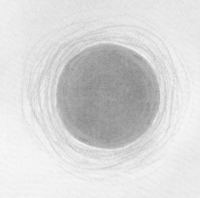

A little while later, the chap with the cane
Looked up and cried, "Gosh! It's those thieves with my plane!"

He ran to the field and leapt over the gate,
Stared all around and sighed,

For there was the bright yellow flying machine,
But the thieves in white sweaters were not to be seen.

There were only some sheep, who were munching away
Just as they always did, day after day.